NOD ROG

In dedication to
Gordon Woodgate

little bee books

New York, NY
Copyright © 2021 by Harry Woodgate
All rights reserved, including the right of reproduction
in whole or in part in any form.
Manufactured in China RRD 1120
First U.S. Edition
1 3 5 7 9 10 8 6 4 2
Library of Congress Cataloging-in-Publication Data is available upon request.
ISBN 978-1-4998-1193-3
Originally printed in the UK by Andersen Press Ltd.
littlebeebooks.com
For more information about special discounts on bulk purchases,
please contact Little Bee Books at sales@littlebeebooks.com.

A PROUD PARTNERSHIP BETWEEN

glaad + little bee books

A portion of the proceeds from the sale of this
book will be donated to accelerating
LGBTQ acceptance.

Grandad's Camper

Harry Woodgate

little bee books

Every summer, I go to stay at my grandad's house by the sea. It's a pretty, old cottage . . .

with bookshelves packed to the brim with
interesting things from Grandad's travels,

and lots of great places to play hide-and-seek!

In the garden, Grandad grows
all kinds of fruits and vegetables.

There's a big cherry tree,
which if you shake just enough . . . *Yum!*

But my favorite thing to do at Grandad's house is
snuggle up on the sofa and listen as Grandad tells me about
all of the amazing places he and Gramps would explore.

"Your gramps was quite the adventurer!

He was tall and handsome,

and excellent at so many things. . . .

Tidiness was not one of them!

"Soon after we met, he invited me on vacation with him,

so we set off in his camper to the seaside.

In the daytime we surfed,

ate fish and chips,

and had a sandcastle competition. . . .

I think I won!

"In the evenings, we'd
have bonfires on the beach

and watch the tide going
in and out of the bay.

One afternoon, Gramps
said to me, 'There are so many
wonderful things in this world, and
I want to see them all with you.'
So, that's exactly what we did.

"Gramps always wanted
to visit the city, so that's
where we went first.

We drove through dark tunnels, over fancy bridges,

and in between towering skyscrapers.

"Everywhere we went was full of life—there were so many people,

so many animals, and so many things to see.

It was amazing.

We saw lots of different kinds of homes,

from high-rise apartments

to town houses.

But we were happy with our little home on wheels, which we could take wherever we pleased."

Grandad puts down his photo album and smiles. I can see how
much he loves those memories and how much he loved Gramps.

"Why don't you go anywhere now, Grandad?"

"It's not the same without Gramps—he made everything feel extra-special. Since Gramps died, I just don't feel like it."

A thought pops into my head. "Do you still have your camper van?" He winks. "Follow me!"

I run outside to the garage
and with all my might,
heave open the big old doors. . . .

There it is! It looks
broken down, but I come up
with a clever plan.

"Let's fix it up and go to the seaside together!"
He looks at me and laughs.
"I suppose it might be nice to take another trip."

Off comes the dust cover and we get started.

Finally, we stand back and look at our handiwork.

"Your gramps would be so happy to see this. It's what he would have wanted. Let's pack some snacks and hot chocolate and then camp on the beach—just like Gramps and I used to!"

So, that's exactly what we do.